Sophie's Masterpiece

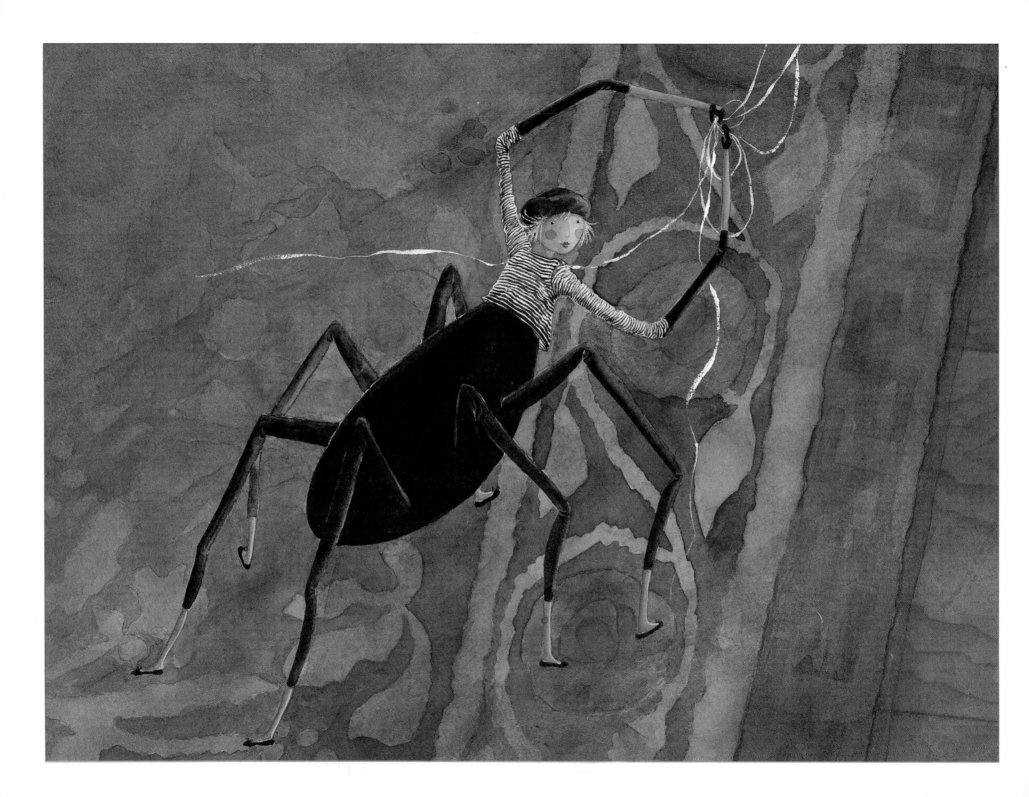

2001 11 22

Sophie's Masterpiece

A Spider's Tale

by EILEEN SPINELLI   illustrations by JANE DYER

17030/

Simon & Schuster Books for Young Readers

NEW YORK   LONDON   TORONTO   SYDNEY   SINGAPORE

SIMON & SCHUSTER BOOKS FOR YOUNG READERS
An imprint of Simon & Schuster Children's Publishing Division
1230 Avenue of the Americas, New York, New York 10020

Book design by Paul Zakris
The text for this book is set in 16-point Calligraphic 810.
The illustrations are rendered on Waterford 140-pound H. P.
paper with Winsor & Newton watercolors.
Printed in United States of America
2 4 6 8 10 9 7 5 3
Library of Congress Cataloging-in-Publication Data
Spinelli, Eileen.
Sophie's masterpiece / by Eileen Spinelli ; pictures by Jane Dyer.
- 1st ed.
p. cm.
Summary: Sophie the spider makes wondrous webs, but the residents of Beekman's Boardinghouse
do not appreciate her until at last, old and tired, she weaves her final masterpiece.
ISBN 0-689-80112-2
[1. Spiders-Fiction. 2. Boardinghouses-Fiction.] I. Dyer, Jane, ill. II. Title.
PZ7.S7566Sr 1998
[E]-dc20 95-44063

To Mary and Tony M.
and Jennifer D.
who love spiders,
and to Eileen G.
who (except for Sophie) doesn't
—E. S.

To Marilyn Marlow, with love
—J. D.

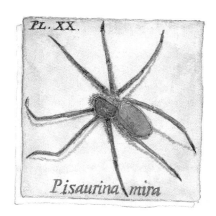

PL. XX.

Pisaurina mira

Sophie was no ordinary house spider.

Sophie was an artist.

She spun webs more wondrous than anyone had ever seen.
Her playmates called her incredible. Her mama was proud.

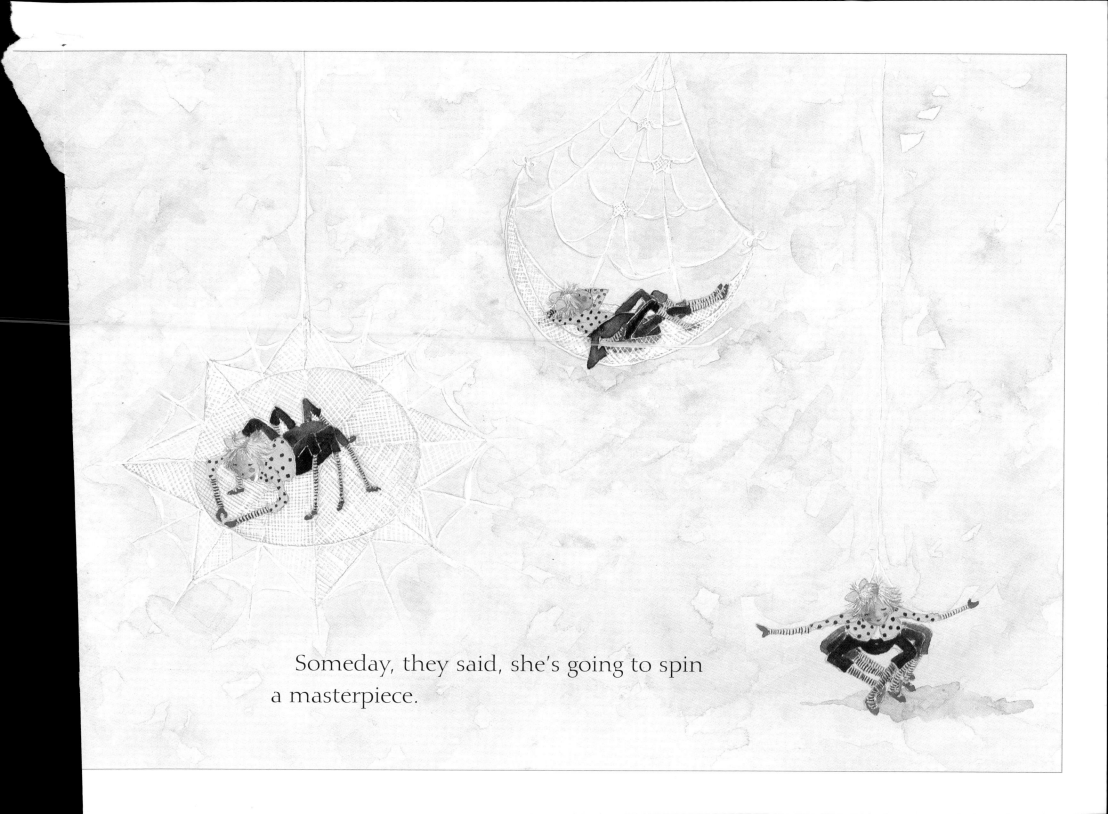

Someday, they said, she's going to spin
a masterpiece.

When Sophie arrived at that age when a young spider must
strike out on her own, she moved to Beekman's Boardinghouse.

The first thing she did was look around. She saw dull green walls, faded rugs, and old window shades. The place cried out for her talents.

Sophie set to work. Her first project was to weave a web of curtains for Beekman's front parlor.

Day after day she whizzed along, blending a golden thread of sun into her silk.

Then one day the landlady noticed her and screamed, "I'll have no spiders in my parlor!" She swatted at Sophie with a dust rag.

Sophie knew when she wasn't wanted. She scampered across the wall and up the stairs into the tugboat captain's closet.

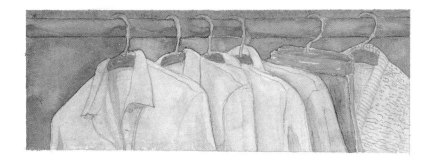

When she finally settled down, she looked around and saw nothing but gray. Gray shirts. Gray pants. Gray sweaters.

The captain needs a new suit, Sophie decided. *Something bright. Blue. Like sky.* She began to spin patiently. A sleeve. A collar.

One day the tugboat captain caught Sophie at work.

He screeched, "A spider!"

Then he climbed onto the windowsill and out to the roof.

Sophie did not want anyone falling off the roof on her account. She scuttled out of the closet, down the hall, and into the cook's bedroom slipper.

Cook's bedroom slippers were patched and dirty.

I'll spin Cook a new pair, Sophie thought. *After I rest a bit.*

No sooner had Sophie snuggled into the toe, than she was being flung to the floor.

Was it an earthquake?

No.

It was Cook who had shaken Sophie out. "Yuck!" scowled Cook. "Look at that ugly, disgusting spider."

Sophie's feelings were hurt. With great dignity she journeyed across the rug and under Cook's door. She made the long, long climb up the steep stairs to the third floor where a young woman lived. Wearily Sophie slipped into the young woman's knitting basket and fell asleep.

By this time, many spider years had passed. Sophie was older. She only had energy to spin a few small things for herself . . . a tiny rose-patterned case for her pillow, eight colorful socks to keep her legs warm.

But mostly she slept.

Then one day the young woman discovered Sophie.

Oh, no, thought Sophie, close to tears. She knew she did not have the strength for any more journeys.

But the young woman did not swat at Sophie with a dust rag.

She did not climb on the roof.

She did not say that Sophie was ugly.

She simply smiled.

And without disturbing Sophie in the least, the young woman picked up her needle and yarn.

Sophie watched as the young woman knitted, day after day.

"Booties!" cried Sophie.

The young woman was going to have a baby.

After the booties were finished, the young woman knitted a baby sweater.

Then the yarn was gone.

The young woman did not have enough money to buy yarn for a baby blanket.

"Never mind," the landlady told her. "There's an old brown quilt in the hall closet. Your baby can use that."

Sophie had seen that quilt. It was scratchy and drab. Not fit for a baby.

Sophie knew the answer. She would have to spin a blanket herself.

In her younger days, this would not have been a problem. But Sophie had grown frail and weak. The baby was due any day. Could Sophie complete the blanket in time?

She climbed out of the yarn basket.

She traveled to the wide windowsill.

Strands of moonlight fell into the room. *Excellent!* she thought. *I'll weave those strands into the baby's blanket. Some starlight, too.*

Sophie began. As she spun, new ideas came to her. She worked them into the blanket . . . snippets of fragrant pine . . . wisps of night . . . old lullabies . . . playful snowflakes. . . .

Sophie spun without blinking.
Or eating.
Or sleeping.
She was never more exhausted. Or determined.
On and on she spun.

She was down to the farthest corner of the blanket when she heard the cry of the young woman's newborn baby. And there, on that farthest corner, is where Sophie wove into the blanket her very own heart.

That night as the young woman was about to cover her infant with the landlady's quilt, something on the windowsill caught her eye.

It was a blanket, so soft, so beautiful as to be fit for a prince.

The young woman knew this was no ordinary blanket.

She placed it with love and wonderment around her sleeping baby.

And went to sleep herself with her hand upon the little spider's last spinning.

Sophie's masterpiece.

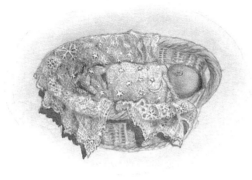

The End